Joshua's Dream

Joshua's Dream
A Journey to the Land of Israel

by Sheila F. Segal

•

illustrated by Joel Iskowitz

UAHC Press
New York, New York

For *Joshua* and *Eli*
as their stories continue

Library of Congress Cataloging-in-Publication Data
Segal, Sheila F.
   Joshua's dream : a journey to the Land of Israel / by Sheila F.
Segal ; illustrated by Joel Iskowitz. — Rev. ed.
       p.   cm.
   Summary: Joshua's dream of taking part in the transformation of
Israel's desert land finally comes true.
   ISBN 0-8074-0476-4 (alk. paper) : $10.95
   [1. Israel—Fiction.]   I. Iskowitz, Joel, ill.   II. Title.
PZ7.S4528Jo   1992
[E]—dc20   91-45513
                                                     CIP
                                                     AC

Manufactured in the United States of America
9 8 7 6 5 4 3 2 1

FELDMAN LIBRARY

THE FELDMAN LIBRARY FUND was created in 1974 through a gift from the Milton and Sally Feldman Foundation. The Feldman Library Fund, which provides for the publication by the UAHC of selected outstanding Jewish books and texts, memorializes Sally Feldman, who in her lifetime devoted herself to Jewish youth and Jewish learning. Herself an orphan and brought up in an orphanage, she dedicated her efforts to helping Jewish young people get the educational opportunities she had not enjoyed.

In loving memory of my beloved wife Sally
"She was my life, and she is gone;
She was my riches, and I am a pauper."

"Many daughters have done valiantly,
but thou excellest them all."

MILTON E. FELDMAN

"Tell me again about Great-Aunt Rivka," Joshua said to his mother. One of his favorite stories was about his grandfather's sister, who went to Israel as a young woman to help make the desert bloom. Joshua thought that was amazing.

Joshua's mother took the old family photograph album out of the cabinet and pulled some big picture books about Israel off the shelf. Joshua climbed up on the sofa next to her.

"Once upon a time, but not very long ago," she always began as she opened one of the books, "the Land of Israel had so many sandy deserts, murky swamps, and rocky hills that hardly any trees, flowers, or food could grow there. And that made it very hard for people to live there.

"For a long time the Jews who lived in the Land of Israel had very little food or money. But they loved their homeland so much that they stayed, they worked hard, and they prayed for better times.

"Then, almost a hundred years ago, many Jews who lived in Europe, the United States, and other countries held a big meeting. They decided to do everything they could to make Eretz Yisrael, the Land of Israel, a better place for Jews to live. They called themselves 'Zionists' because in the Bible 'Zion' was another name for the Land of Israel. Many Zionists, like Aunt Rivka, packed up and went to Israel to help make that dream come true."

"But how could they make things grow in the desert?" Joshua asked.

"Well, it took a lot of new ideas, a lot of courage, and a lot of hard work," his mother said. "Many people did not believe that it was possible, but before long the Zionist settlers began to make miracles happen.

5

"They brought water to the desert through new pipes and sprinklers, so that orange trees could grow in the sandy earth.

"They drained the swamps and planted seeds, so that animals could graze on new grass.

"They blasted away rocks, so that date palms and almond trees and flowers could grow along hillsides.

10

11

"And they built a city by the sea on dunes of sand."

13

"And Aunt Rivka did some of those things—right, Mom?"
Joshua said proudly.

"She sure did," his mother said. "Aunt Rivka was brave and strong, and she believed in her dreams. So in 1906, when she was only twenty years old, she went to Israel to help start a tiny farming village. There she slept in a tent and worked all day in the hot sun—digging, clearing, planting, and watering—until she saw her dreams begin to come true: orange trees growing in the desert, children playing in their shade and eating their fruit.

"As the years passed Aunt Rivka's village grew, and Israel became a strong country with more people and more trees each year.

16

"In Israel today Jews are still moving to the desert wilderness and the rocky hills to make them bloom with new trees and to build new villages full of people."

17

"One day," Joshua thought, "I'm also going to help build Israel, with my own hands, like Aunt Rivka."

Joshua spent a lot of time looking at the books about Israel. He paid special attention to pictures of people working in the desert so that, when the time came, he could make sure to bring everything he needed—a hat to shade him from the hot sun, work shorts, sturdy shoes, a canteen for drinking water, and of course a good shovel for digging and planting.

Then one day his mother surprised him. "Pack up your gear," she said. "We'll all be off to Israel next week."

Joshua was thrilled. Now he could see himself standing in the desert with sand all around him, digging up the earth with his own tools, setting a little tree into the ground with his own hands.

And that's just what he did.

One hot and windy morning in June, Joshua stood at the edge of a small forest, right in the middle of the Negev Desert. The forest was only three years old, but already there were a thousand trees. Many of them were very tall.

22

The forester, who guards the forest and takes care of the trees, gave Joshua a tiny Jerusalem pine tree.

"We grow the trees in our nursery for almost one year," the forester told Joshua, "until they are strong enough to be brought outside. This one is just ready for planting, and here's a good spot."

Joshua put his hands around the little tree—the smallest tree he had ever seen. He held it proudly for a few moments. Then gently he put it down beside him. With his shovel he dug a hole in the dry and rocky soil. Next, he carefully set the little tree into the hole he had made for it.

The tree wobbled in the wind as Joshua scooped up the soil with his shovel and placed some of it around and over the roots. Then, with his hands, he piled more sand around the base and patted it down until the little tree stood steadily against the wind, ready to live and grow in the outdoors.

"I did it!" he laughed as he jumped to his feet. "This little tree will grow in the desert, and I planted it!" It really was his dream come true—his own part in building the Land of Israel. And he knew even then that one day he would come back to do much more.

From that time on, whenever his mother took out the family album and the picture books to tell the story about Aunt Rivka and the builders of Israel, Joshua also was a part of it. But his own story was just beginning.

Joshua Segal, age 4, planting his first tree in Israel